MR. CAREY'S GARDEN

MR. CAREY'S GARDEN

by Jane Cutler • *pictures by* G. Brian Karas

Houghton Mifflin Company
Boston 1996

For information about this and other Houghton Mifflin
trade and reference books and multimedia products,
visit The Bookstore at Houghton Mifflin on the
World Wide Web at http://www.hmco.com/trade/.

Manufactured in the United States of America

Book design by David Saylor
The text of this book is set in 16-point Minister Book.
The illustrations are gouache, acrylic, and pencil, reproduced in full color.

WOZ 10 9 8 7 6 5 4 3 2 1

LIBRARY OF CONGRESS CATALOGING-IN-PUBLICATION DATA
Cutler, Jane.
Mr. Carey's garden / written by Jane Cutler ;
illustrated by G. Brian Karas. p. cm.
Summary: All of his neighbors have suggestions for how to get rid
of the snails in his garden, but Mr. Carey isn't interested.
ISBN 0-395-68191-X
[1. Gardens—Fiction. 2. Snails—Fiction] I. Karas, G. Brian, ill.
II. Title: Mister Carey's garden. PZ7.C985Mr 1996
[E]—dc20 93-13720 CIP AC

FOR JOHN SCHINDEL

—J. C.

FOR MARILYN

—G. B. K.

Down at the end of Blackberry Lane live four people who love their gardens. In some ways the gardens are alike. But each garden has something remarkable about it, something that makes it different from the others.

Mr. Munsing has watermelons.
Seedless watermelons, he says.

Ms. Elwood has a milk-fed pumpkin that's so big she can't lift it by herself.

Mr. Febold has sunflowers that stand taller than he does.

And Mr. Carey has plants that are full of holes.

"It's snails," Mr. Munsing tells Mr. Carey. "Do them the way I do. Creep out in the dark with a flashlight and a bag of salt. Pluck them off the plants and sprinkle them. They'll shrivel up to nothing and trouble you no more."

Mr. Carey listens. “I appreciate your suggestion,” he says. “But I see it in a different light.”

Later, Ms. Elwood comes by.

"Snails?" she says. "Do them the way I do. Get up at first light and gather your harvest of snails. Then put them in a plastic bag and stick them in the freezer. Frozen snails. They'll trouble you no more."

"I appreciate your suggestion," Mr. Carey tells her. "But I see it in a different light."

Toward evening, Mr. Febold walks by.

"Do them the way I do," Mr. Febold says. "Poison the pests. They'll trouble you no more."

Mr. Carey studies the box of poison pellets. "Thing is," he tells Mr. Febold, "I see it in a different light."

The puzzled neighbors buzz. They don't understand what Mr. Carey means.

Until one summer night.

This summer night is warm and still and filled with the light of the full moon floating high in the sky and beaming down so enthusiastically that nobody at the end of Blackberry Lane can sleep a wink.

Mr. Munsing brews himself a whole pot of Sleep Tight Tea and drinks it all.

When that doesn't work, he puts on his plaid bathrobe and his carpet slippers and goes outside for a breath of air.

Ms. Elwood counts a thousand imaginary sheep jumping over an imaginary fence.

When that doesn't help, she puts on her dressing gown and her scuffs and goes out for a midnight stroll.

Mr. Febold reads the telephone book backward.

When that's no use, he puts on his wraparound and his flip-flops and decides to walk to the corner and back.

A soft, steady sound, the sound of nibbling and crunching, draws Mr. Munsing, Ms. Elwood, and Mr. Febold down to the end of the block.

When they come to Mr. Carey's garden, they stop and stare.

They stare at stately snails crisscrossing
Mr. Carey's garden, at their glistening trails
that shine like silver ribbons in the moonlight.

They stare at the broad, gnawed leaves of the plants throwing lacy shadows on the ground.

Now they see the garden in a different light.

Same as Mr. Carey does.

They stare at Mr. Carey, sitting on his porch and looking with pleasure at the magical place his garden has become.

Now whenever the night is warm and still and the moon is high and full, the people who live down at the end of Blackberry Lane come to sit with Mr. Carey on his porch and watch the snails glide back and forth in the moonlight.